fish, fog, frogs

(and other stories)

by Jackie Lutes

Illustrated by
Jennifer and Jonathan Goldstein

Fish, Fog, Frogs
and
Other Stories

To the many
milies of Gould Farm
o have collectively created
family/community that is
ld Farm. May each of you be
spired* to identify your own
tories." Thank you for welcoming
into your family for a brief
t never to be forgotten visit.

Jackie Linehan felder
3/30/14

*(perhaps best to read p. 79 before reading the stories)

Table of Contents

Dedication vii

Chapter One
The Big Round Table 1

Chapter Two
Same Table, New Audience 7

Chapter Three

A Fish Tale 13

Chapter Four
North Woods Weather 23

Chapter Five
A Close Call for Horse 31

Chapter Six
How Cold Was It?.. 39

Chapter Seven
Another Bear! 47

Chapter Eight

The Trouble with Fog 53

Chapter Nine

My Striped Blazer... 61

Chapter Ten

The Closer 71

Epilogue... 79
Acknowledgments... 81

Dedication

June 18, 1910 - July 13, 1980

John R. Lutes – Jack, Daddy, Pops, Uncle Jack, Gaga. These were some of the affectionate tags to which he responded, a man of many names with a personality that included many traits. He had a quick temper and a sensitive forgiving nature. He was a harsh disciplinarian and an indulgent benefactor. He was a hard realist and a creative child.

He was here for 70 years, yet it seemed he left too soon. But, to those who knew him well he will never be gone. People such as Daddy – people who live life to the fullest, who are never bored or boring, who plunge forward, sometimes stumbling, more often triumphant - these people are not forgotten. Daddy left many legacies but the one that is clearest in my memory, which I loved the most, was his ability to spontaneously tell imaginative stories.

The following collection is a fond memory for those of us who experienced him and an introduction to those who were not so fortunate. While I can never reproduce the special charm that he gave to his stories, I have tried to retell them in his style – a style that was characterized by humorous digressions, a warm confidentiality and a nonsensical logic that gave you permission to believe (or dared you *not* to believe). There is a child in all of us, sometimes buried too deeply, that longs to play and be free, to be unleashed from understanding and explanation. For me, Daddy's stories allowed that child to come out and play. I hope that all who read this will in their own way share that kind of experience.

In loving memory of my father, the real author of this book,

Jackie Lutes Goldstein

Chapter One
The Big Round Table

When our parents talk to us of the good old days, they often don't sound that good, only old. I could never see anything exciting or "good" about shoveling coal in the wee morning hours or trudging five miles to and from school through "at least" six feet of snow, uphill both ways. However, there was one brand of story that my father, Daddy, would tell that pleased not only my brother and me but any visiting friends who were lucky enough to share in our after-dinner family time sitting with us at the dinner table, a big round table with curved Queen Ann legs and a story of its own.

When Mother bought the used table, for $1.00, it wore at least one chipped and shabby coat of paint. Some years later, with no room in the budget for a professional refinisher, Mother, with loving labor, removed the layers of paint and transformed that table. It became *the* dining table at every one of our homes thereafter – until Mother and Daddy enjoyed success in their family-owned business. Then the table was treated to some professional cosmetics and enjoyed executive status as the conference table in Daddy's office. Nevertheless, the big round table's best days (its most remembered purpose) were was when it was a place for Daddy to drink coffee and do the morning crossword puzzle, as well as a place for Mother and Daddy to play chess after dinner and, of course, as *the* place for after-dinner conversation and laughter and Daddy's stories, imaginative tales that delighted me into my college years.

Even when college friends came home with me for a weekend visit, if I could convince Daddy to share his stories (not a difficult selling job), they loved his brand of entertainment. It wasn't just the imaginative content of the stories that made them popular. It wasn't just the nonsensical logic that drew one's attention. It was the casual, chatty way in which he delivered the stories, commonly sipping on his coffee as he told the story, often pausing to ask Mother for a refill, with the pauses deliberately timed for story-telling effect.

Also, in "those days" people fixed things that today we would probably throw away, and Daddy enjoyed this kind of "puttering." So, if a radio or a lamp or an electric razor needed some work, Daddy welcomed the opportunity to putter at the big round table. Yet, even if he was involved in a fix-it task, the puttering didn't stop when he gave in to a plea for stories; he could multi-task, still pausing now and then to run his hand over his bald head while he waited for a coffee refill. The coffee-sipping and head-rubbing pauses were effectively timed and placed, leaving his audience eager for him to continue.

Indeed, he knew how to hold an audience's attention. In fact, he spent most of his working life as a salesman and I'm betting he used the same "pause and make them wonder what's coming next" approach with his customers. After all, a successful salesman simply knows how to tell an appealing and convincing story about his product. Given his success as a salesman, telling a story was surely a talent that served him well. When he was telling stories at the big round table, he was "selling" the idea of a world of imagination. Same story teller. Same talent. Different setting. Different product.

Chapter Two
Same Table, New Audience

After two years in college, followed by two years working at a local insurance company, I left home for a more exciting and independent life as a flight attendant. However, I seemed to be on the "two-year plan" because, after two years flying around the country (while I served full course meals to *all* passengers, even during relatively short flights – and that is not a tall tale; it's truly the "good old days" of flying), I married a handsome and charming passenger (also a salesman). I moved to a faraway state (his home state) where we bought a home and, one year later, began our family with the birth of Jennifer. In another three years, Jonathan, who Jennifer designated as "the new baby," joined the family.

In our home, with my new family, there was a den where we often watched TV after dinner. There was a nice patio outside the den that got heavy "sitting around" use in nice weather. When Jonathan was one-year old, we added a "play room" for the children and their visiting friends. But there was no big table, round or otherwise, where we lingered after dinner. Daddy's story telling tradition became little more than a memory.

Though we lived 600 miles from my family (and the big round table), we still visited my family and the table once or twice a year. It was on one of those visits, as we sat around the table after dinner, that the stories once again popped into my mind like old friends suddenly remembered. And here sat my two children who, just as I had at one time, frowned at recollections of the "good old days." But they did appreciate Gaga's humor and, given the talents of their grandfather, could it possibly be that they would find the same fun in these stories that I and my friends had found years before? I smiled as I thought that *maybe* I could once again show off my talented father and decided to give it a try.

"Daddy, tell the kids the story about the pet fish that you used to have."

He appeared to have forgotten (more likely only pretending to forget in order to prompt some urging). For a moment he looked puzzled, and then it all came back to him (or, again, he pretended that it all came back to him). Whether his forgetfulness was real or a bit of subtle drama, the years between my love of Daddy's story telling and what I hoped would be my children's love of the same stories were erased. And his story-telling sales tricks began, as he smiled and shyly said, "Oh, they wouldn't want to hear about that." (An obvious "trick," for John R. Lutes was not shy!)

"I know they would. Come on. Tell them," I urged.

He sighed, "Well, alright. But it's pretty sad, you know."

The children were surely wondering how a pet fish story could even be interesting, let alone sad, but they enjoyed their grandfather's sense of humor and, perhaps suspecting they were going to get a taste of it, they showed Gaga proper respect and, in spite of a little squirming, prepared to listen. I settled in with a big smile on my face, and in my heart, as *I* prepared to once again enjoy my favorite big round table tradition.

Chapter Three
A Fish Tale

Both Daddy and Mother knew the routine and as he prepared to start, she brought him a fresh cup of coffee while he ran his hand over his now even balder head. In fact, he now just shaved his entire head. He claimed that, with so little hair, the barber was charging a "finder's fee" and, to save money, he would personally just extend his daily face shaving to a whole head shave.

Once the coffee was served, he took a sip, leaned back in his chair, looked as if he was collecting his thoughts, and the fun began. . .

"When I was a kid I spent a lot of time up in the area of Dad's resort in Northern Minnesota, and I used to do quite a bit of fishing. On one of my North woods fishing trips I caught a very small speckled trout. He was too small to eat, but I thought I'd keep him anyway; fatten him up and within a few months, he'd make a nice trout dinner for me.

14

"Well, I took him home in a bucket, put him in an old fish bowl that we had left over from a goldfish I'd won at a carnival, and I hurried down to the store and bought some regular goldfish food – the flake kind.

"As time went by I got pretty attached to the little fellow and even gave him a name – Fish. Not too original but pretty descriptive. He was really smart as fish go, and I used to hold one of those fish food flakes above the water and holler, 'Fish, Fish, Fish!', and he'd come and take it right out of my hand. Cutest thing you ever did see."

Daddy took another sip of coffee, settled into his chair and looked like he was enjoying the experience of remembering his pet as much as he was enjoying his role as story teller / salesman. But, after a pause, he continued.

"I'll tell you just how smart Fish was. One weekend the family went on a three-day trip. The first night we were gone, a burglar broke into the house and stole all of our family silver and Mother's beautiful Persian lamb jacket. Well, the burglar apparently had some inside information and knew we were gone for the weekend. It appears that he wasn't

16

in a big hurry, so he must have stopped to look at Fish and dropped one of those fish flakes in his bowl. At least he was a kind, animal-loving burglar. But Fish was too smart to fall for this guy's kind side. He knew something wasn't right, that this guy didn't belong in our house. So, he quickly grabbed the flake before it hit the water and held it out of the water until we got home. We took that flake down to the police station; they got the fingerprints off of it and arrested the thief that very day."

"Oh, Gaga," Jennifer asked, "Is that really true?"

"Of course it is. You just ask your mother if she remembers her grandmother's Persian lamb jacket. She'll remember."

"But Gaga . . . "

"Besides, he was awarded the Fish-of-the-Year Medal for that deed. Now, where was I . . . ? Oh, yes. . . This was one smart fish. I would take him out of the water for a few minutes every day, keeping him out a little longer each time. Finally, he got so that I could lay him on the floor beside me and he'd flop along behind as I walked through the house. Eventually, we even ventured out of the house and used to take long walks together. You don't really want to hear the rest of this, do you? It's just too sad."

"Come on, Gaga – please! What happened?" The kids had learned how to play the game and were as cooperative as they were curious.

"Oh, alright. But, I always get kind of teary when I tell it," said Daddy, knowing that he was feeding their curiosity and the suspense.

"Well, one day, after a light rain, we were taking our daily afternoon walk. We were going across this little foot bridge that went over a small stream when Fish slipped on a wet spot, fell into the stream and drowned.

"I think that is one of the saddest memories of my young life. I had even started teaching him to talk. He was making little squeaks already, and I had great hopes of teaching him some words and maybe even a nursery rhyme or two."

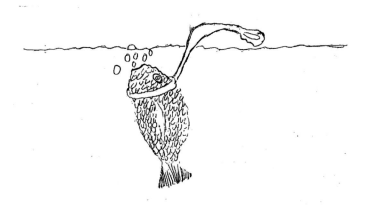

By now Daddy was really into the drama of the moment and was fully enjoying the spot light. He put on his far-away nostalgic look as he said, "Yes, those were some good old days up in those North woods. We sure had some great times. . ."

I knew how the game was played and that they should now ask about those "great times." I silently cheered Jennifer's intuitive understanding of the rules as I heard her say, "Please, Gaga, tell us some more."

"Oh, I'm sure you kids have better things to do," said Daddy. But, without further pause he was off again, into the next story in his collection.

Chapter Four
North Woods Weather

"We spent a lot of winters and all of our summers up in that area – from Grand Marais, up the Gunflint Trail, all the way up to Lake Wasigon by the Ontario-Quatskow Provincial Park at the Canadian border.

"It's beautiful country but the climate there is kind of weird. They would have quick thaws and quick freezes and you never knew when one of those things was coming. A quick freeze was called a Chinook. This is where it would be warm one minute and the next minute so cold that your words could freeze in midair. If someone were talking to you and a Chinook set in smack dab in the middle of a sentence, you would have to wait for a quick thaw to find out what the end of the sentence was.

"Anyway, one spring day a friend of mine, Jim Krill, and I went up to Lowey Lake, which was always full of frogs. We kind of had a taste for a frog leg dinner. You know frogs' legs are a real delicacy

24

– cost you a bunch in a fine restaurant – but once in a while we'd get lucky and catch ourselves some.

"Now when frogs are floating, the tops of their heads stick out of the water and not much shows but their eyes. When they dive, they put their heads down and for just a fraction of a second their legs stick straight up out of the water. The day Jim and I were up there the lake was just covered with floating frogs. Nothing but frogs' eyes for as far as you could see. Then, apparently, they felt one of those quick-freeze Chinooks coming because all at once they dove for the bottom of the lake. But, they were just a little too slow and, as they started to dive, the Chinook hit. All the way across that whole lake, as far as you could see, there was nothing but frogs' legs sticking straight up in the air out of the ice. What a sight!

"Well, we did some real fast thinking – Jim and I did – and ran to a nearby cabin that belonged to Jim's uncle. We got an old lawn mower with a canvas grass catcher on the back and hurried back to the lake before the quick thaw set in. Lucky for us it was slow in coming because all the rest of the day we went back and forth across that lake mowing frogs' legs. I don't remember exactly how many we got, but we had ourselves a nice big frogs' leg dinner and took the rest down to a fancy restaurant in Duluth. We sold them to that restaurant and got about a hundred dollars, which was a small fortune in those days.

"To this day at Lake Lowey in Minnesota the frogs have no legs. I know it sounds odd, but it's just one of those freak facts of nature. If you're ever up that way, you can check it out."

Chapter Five
A Close Call for Horse

By now Daddy was so involved in his memories and imagination (and his place in the spotlight) that he even forgot to be coaxed into the next story. As he motioned to Mother for another cup of coffee, I was pretty sure that we were going to hear the whole North Woods adventure series.

"We got ourselves a pretty good horse with some of that money and used to have some really good times roaming around up there - just Jim, me and Horse. Yeah, we just called him Horse. I never was very good at coming up with names for animals. Guess I don't have much imagination." (I saw him smile as he "confessed" his lack of imagination, and I am pretty sure he winked at me as he said it.)

"The next winter was the winter of the big snow, of course. I've never seen so much snow in my entire life. That was the winter that Lake Ontario was formed, you know. Before that there were only. four Great Lake But there was so much snow that they didn't know what to do with it so they just kept piling it over on the Michigan-Canadian border. That pile got pretty high, and, when the whole thing melted in the spring, it just settled right down and became what we now call Lake Ontario. Now you *know* that's true, because you can see Lake Ontario on any map or globe.

"Anyway, Jim and I were young and we weren't going to let a little snow slow us down. So, one day we decided to go to a little neighboring town called Tofften. You'll find it on any Minnesota map just north of Grand Marais. Before we left, we stopped by a little Indian Trading Post where they made some fine snowshoes.

"We had some made for us and for Horse and we were on our way. We had our sleeping bags tied to the back of Horse and had plenty of beef jerky and some matches to melt the snow for drinking. You had to be prepared to spend the night out when you left home in that kind of weather.

"It was usually only about a half a day's ride to Toffton, but in that weather, it took us until almost sundown to get where we thought Toffton should be. But, visibility wasn't so good with all that snow coming down.

"Well, when we got where we figured Toffton was supposed to be, there wasn't a sign of anything that looked the least bit like civilization. All we could see was a really tall pole sticking out of the snow. We were pretty tired – and cold – so we tied Horse to the pole, had us a little snack, and settled into our sleeping bags for the night. (We had also brought along a blanket and some feed for Horse, so all three of us were about as comfortable as we could be, under the circumstances.)

"Apparently during the night one of those quick thaws set in, because when we woke up in the morning the snow was gone and we were sleeping on the front porch of a church, but Horse was nowhere to be seen. Finally, one of us looked up when we thought we heard a neighing coming from above us and, sure enough, there was Horse hanging by his harness from the flagpole on top of the church steeple.

"It took us a few minutes to figure out how to get ourselves out of that predicament. (Or rather, how to get Horse out of *his* predicament.) Fortunately, I had a pistol along (in case of any wild animal attacks). I was known to be a pretty good shot and Jim was one of the strongest guys around those parts. So, we came up with a plan to rescue Horse. I took out my .45 and aimed at the rope. My shot was right on target, as usual; the rope broke, Horse dropped down, right into Jim's arms, and Jim very gently placed him on the ground. Our plan worked perfectly.

"Neither Jim nor Horse was hurt. But, by gosh, Horse never would go near another flagpole for as long as he traveled with us.

"And, by the way, I was talking to an old friend from those parts the other day, and he tells me there's still a chunk of rope hanging from the steeple of Lake Superior Lutheran in Toffton."

Chapter Six
How Cold Was It?

Laughs were shared, appropriate comments made, more coffee poured for Daddy, milk for the kids, cookies passed around the table, and we all settled in for more stories as Jonathan asked, "Was it really cold the winter of the big snow, Gaga?"

"Oh boy – you can't believe how cold it was. It was the bitter cold that led to one of the most unusual experiences that I ever had.

"It must have gotten down around 70, 80, 90 below zero that winter. But, like I said, I was young and nothing stopped me. So, one day I decided to go on a bear hunt. My dad owned several rifles and, since I was very careful with guns, he would let me use any of them. For some reason this day I took a muzzle loader even though it was not really one of my favorites. (But it did turn out to be a good choice, as you'll see.) I had hunted most of the morning and hadn't done a single thing except use up all of my lead balls, but I still had a lot of powder left.

I decided to head for home and hadn't gone too far when out from behind a tree comes the biggest, meanest bear I, or probably anyone else, had ever seen. I had plenty of powder in the gun and, for a split second, I got excited at the prospect of bringing home a bear of that size. Of course, my excitement was short-lived as I remembered that I was out of ammunition! Well, that bear started coming at me and I took off running so fast that my shadow couldn't keep up with me. I was so scared that, cold as it was, the perspiration was pouring off of my forehead, but as it came out, the drops instantly formed into ice balls.

"I knew that I had to think fast and luckily, as I was running, a brilliant idea flashed into my mind. As I ran, I took those little ice balls off of my forehead and jammed them down into the rifle barrel on top of the powder. For my plan to succeed my timing had to be perfect, and I was ready to do what I needed to do. All of a sudden I stopped dead in my tracks and instantly turned around. The bear was only a few feet away and I fired my gun at its head – point-blank.

"I had thought that the ice balls would be so hard that they would serve the same purpose as lead balls. Well, my idea was pretty good, except for one thing; as the powder ignited, the heat of the blast melted the ice balls and all that came out of the gun was a stream of water. For half a second I thought I was a goner, but I was saved by the intense cold. The stream of water froze instantly into an icicle as it hit the arctic-like air. My aim was perfect and the icicle struck the bear directly between the eyes and went into his head. Unfortunately, the heat of the bear's body once again melted the ice, and I was sure that now my luck had truly run out.

"Fate took a happy turn for me, though, and the bear did die instantly – of water on the brain."

Chapter Seven
Another Bear!

"I had quite a few close calls with bears. There was another experience that was even more frightening because I didn't have a gun that time. This happened while I was taking a walk in the woods on a beautiful summer day.

"For a long time after I lost Fish I used to take walks in the woods all by my-self and reminisce about our happy days together. I'm sorry that I keep dwelling on that sad event, but sometimes when I think about it I just get real melancholy."

He paused for a sip of coffee and ran his hand over his bald head before continuing. During the pause, the room was silent, as the kids seemed to wonder if Gaga was really sad. By now, they weren't sure what was true and what wasn't, but they seemed to kind of like the experience of wondering.

"Anyway, where was I . . . ? Oh yes, walking alone in the woods . . . when I came on this bear, even bigger and meaner than the other one. (Or she came on me. I guess it doesn't really matter.) Well, I knew that I was going to have to think double fast to get myself out of this one, but I also knew that I was going to have to run triple fast and I decided to do that immediately.

"I was a pretty fast runner in those days – could outrun most of the local horses. (Must have developed that talent when Horse and I would race each other.) *But* . . . as I ran, I looked over my shoulder and that bear was gaining on me fast with her mouth hanging wide open.

"I remembered one bit of information that not too many people know about, and I thought I could use it to my advantage now. Bears are real fast runners but they're mighty slow stoppers. So, I just let her gain on me and then, when she got within an arm's length, I stopped dead in my tracks, spun around and stuck my arm straight out. As she charged at me, I let my rigid arm go into her open mouth and down her throat. I grabbed her on the inside where her tail would be, gave a quick jerk, turned her inside out and she was headed in the other direction.

"That experience must have really shaken her up, because I ran into the same bear a few weeks later. (She had somehow managed to get herself turned right side out by then. Must have gotten help from another bear. I didn't know they were that kind to each other.) She was still sort of mumbling, or growling, to herself and, when she saw me, she instantly took off running in the opposite direction before I even had a chance to be worried.

"Thank goodness – with some quick thinking and a little bit of luck – I always seemed to figure a way out of those bear predicaments."

Chapter Eight
The Trouble with Fog

Daddy segued straight into his next story with, "Boy, we really had some strange weather up there.

"Besides the snow and the famous quick freezes and thaws, we had some really thick fog up there in that North country. And, when I say fog, I mean fog! London is supposed to be famous for its fog. Why, that's kid's stuff compared to the fog that we had. We had fog so thick you could sell it by the pound. Jim and I used to make us a little extra spending money doing exactly that. That was before humidifiers. So mothers would buy our fog and save it until one of their children had the croup. Then they would just open up a few bags and pretty soon the coughing would stop. That was just one of the many uses that people found for our specially packaged fog.

When I was talking to my old friend the other day, he told me that our business is still known as *The Fog Bank*. It's nice to be remembered. Pretty proud of that success.

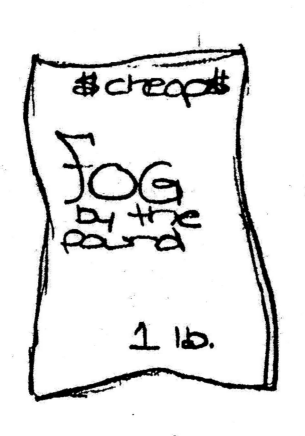

"I remember one particular fog that almost got me into trouble. Dad decided one summer that our lake cabin needed a new roof and I was assigned the job of nailing down the shingles. I wasn't too thrilled about the job because Jim and I had made other plans for the day, but when Dad assigned a job, there was no further discussion – you just did it and you'd better, by gosh, do it well. I was up on the roof putting the shingles across in a row and counting how many shingles to a row. (I used to count everything, and I was pretty good at it, too. When it would rain at night, I used to lie in bed and count the raindrops on the roof until I dozed off. During a real bad rain-storm one night I got up to 1,437,589,956.)

"Well, I was shingling away when all of a sudden one of these thick fogs sets in. I really wanted to finish the job, so I just kept at it in spite of the fog. I was anxious to find Jim so that we could sell a few pounds of the stuff. We hadn't had a good thick fog for a long time and some of our best customers were running low on their supplies. I couldn't see a thing, but I was pretty sure that there were supposed to be 28 shingles to a row. I had been daydreaming, though, so I wasn't too surprised when I got 33 shingles to the remaining rows.

"That particular fog didn't lift until 6:00 the next morning. (Jim and I must have sold at least three or four hundred pounds of the stuff.) Well, about 6:15 in the morning Dad came and woke me up, madder than. . . well, let's just say that he was not one bit happy and I think I heard him say a few words that I *knew* were not spoken by gentlemen (at least, that's what he always told *me*). He was claiming that I hadn't cleaned up after I finished my job. Dad always insisted that a job was not finished until every tool and all the materials were put away. I protested that I had

58

put every leftover shingle and all the tools into the storage space under the cabin."

" 'Well, there sure is a mighty large pile of shingles over by the west end of the cabin,' said Dad.

"I couldn't believe it and went out to see for myself. Sure enough, there lay six feet of shingles side by side – overlapped and nailed as neat as could be. The mystery was solved when I looked at the width of the roof – 28 shingles wide.

"What happened was that the fog was so thick that I had gone three feet past the edge of the roof and nailed five shingles of each row *into* the fog. Of course, when the fog lifted, the shingles fell to the ground.

"Now, I'll put our fog up against that sissy London stuff any day of the week."

Chapter Nine

My Striped Blazer

"You sure spent a lot of time outdoors," remarked Jonathan, a real outdoors boy himself.

"Oh, sure. But we used to get into town and go to dances quite a bit when we got older. When I was in my teens, probably about 18 or 19, back in the roaring twenties, I went to a lot of dances. One dance I'll never forget.

"I had just gotten a brand-new red and white striped blazer and some white pants and I really thought I looked spiffy."

"Spiffy?" we all asked together.

"Yes – spiffy. You know – neato, cool, whatever. There was a pretty cute new girl there who I'd never seen before and we ended up dancing together most of the evening. Her name was Alice Blue. Sometime during the evening I asked her where she lived and she gave me her address. When the dance was over, I asked her if I could give her a ride home and she jumped at the chance. (Hard for you to believe that this old bald grandfather of yours was popular with the girls, huh?)

"My car was a nifty Ford convertible. (Yes, nifty. That's about the same thing as spiffy.) It was a little cool that night so I let Alice put my fancy, striped blazer around her bare shoulders.

"I started to drive her to the address she had given me earlier, but on the way we passed a big cemetery which happened to be right across the street from a theater that your Grandmother worked in when I met her. As we turned the corner by the cemetery Alice asked me if I'd stop. I was kind of puzzled at such a strange request, but, since she asked me, I did pull up to the edge of the cemetery. When I stopped the car, she asked to be excused for a minute. *Now* I was really puzzled, but I was a gentleman, so I just said, 'Certainly,' and she disappeared into the cemetery.

"I sat and waited for at least 15 or 20 minutes and was starting to get concerned – a little bit about Alice and a *lot* about my new red and white striped blazer. Finally, not knowing what else to do, I drove to the address that she had given me. I went to the door, and when I knocked, a man stuck his head out of an upstairs window and asked what I wanted.

" 'I'm looking for Alice Blue,' I called back.

"Even though I could only see him in the window above me, I noticed what looked like stunned shock on his face as he replied, 'You just wait right there, Sonny.'

"So I stood there waiting until at last the door was opened by an elderly gentleman, the one who had stuck his head out the window. I asked if this was the Blue residence. He said that it was and I asked, 'Well, can I see Alice Blue?'

"He looked at me real strange and then quietly and slowly said, 'Just a minute.'

"At that, he called up the stairs, 'Ma, you'd better come down here!'

"An old woman in a flowered bathrobe came sleepily down the steps but immediately became alert when her husband said, 'Ma, this young fella is lookin' for Alice.'

"She studied me a moment and asked, 'How do you know Alice?'

"I impatiently told them the story of our evening together, and ended by explaining how anxious I was to get back my blazer. When they asked if I could describe her, I told them what she looked like and even remembered exactly what she was wearing.

"They looked at each other and then at me for what seemed like forever. Finally, the lady sat down on a chair near the door and the old man, with tears in his eyes, said to me. 'Well, you've described our daughter alright. But, she died six months ago and the dress you described is the dress she was buried in.'

"The whole thing sounded pretty ridiculous to me, but the old couple really seemed shook up, so we all agreed to drive back to the cemetery where I had let Alice out.

"When we got there, Mr. Blue led me to where he said Alice was buried, as his wife followed hesitantly behind us. I still didn't believe them but when we got there, sure enough, there was a small tombstone with the simple inscription: ALICE MARIE BLUE, September 4, 1911 - March 19, 1928. And, hanging on the stone, shining in the light of the full moon, was my red and white striped blazer.

"Boy was I glad to get that blazer back!"

Chapter Ten
The Closer

It was pretty quiet around the big round table for a few minutes. Then, after some puzzled discussion between the kids, Jonathan asked directly, "Gaga, are these stories *really* true? They just couldn't be." But then added, with obvious hopefulness, "Could they?"

In a voice of feigned insult, Daddy answered, "What?! You doubt your grandfather? Why I thought we were good friends, Jonathan."

Jennifer piped in, "But Gaga, they're pretty far out."

"Hmm . . . I can see I'm going to have to tell you one more story.

"One time when I was about nine or 10 years old my grandfather gave me a dime to go to the store and buy whatever my heart desired. A dime was a lot of money then and I was very excited, as there were lots of things that I had been wanting over at the five and ten. (In those days a five and ten-cent store really had items for five and ten cents. Now there's a story that *is* hard to believe.)

"So, I stuck this dime in my knickers pocket and went skipping and whistling down the road, happier than a crow in a cornfield. But, just as I was turning into the store, I tripped and fell, and the precious dime rolled right out of my pocket and landed at the feet of a woman who was coming out of the store. She quickly picked it up and put it straight into her purse without even looking back at me. I couldn't believe my eyes and, while I had been taught to respect my elders, I couldn't help but speak up.

"Ma'am," I said, "that's my dime you picked up."

"She sort of turned up her nose and said, 'Does it have your name on it?'

"I answered, 'No, of course not. But, you saw me fall and you saw it roll out of my pocket.'

"As she walked away, she looked back over her shoulder and I couldn't believe it when I heard her say, 'Finders keepers, losers weepers.'

"Well, we kids said that kind of thing, but I never expected to hear it from a grown woman.

"My pants had been torn and my knee skinned when I fell, but I wasn't going to let that woman out of my sight until I figured a way to get back my dime, so I limped down the street following behind her.

"She was going in and out of a lot of stores and I followed her into one of them, but she told the owner that I was bothering her and he shooed me out. After that I just waited outside at each of her stops, looking for a place to make my move. Finally, as she was coming out of one store, she dropped a package. Here was my chance for revenge. I swooped down and scooped up the package as fast as I could.

"Young man, hand over that package immediately," she demanded.

"Does it have your name on it?" I asked.

"Now you know perfectly well that it doesn't," she answered. "But, you also know that it's mine. You saw me drop it."

"Finders keepers, losers weepers," I hollered over my shoulder and ran as fast as lightening, forgetting about my hurt knee and wondering what was in the package.

"I didn't open it until I was safely in the house and in my room with the door closed. Then I sat down on my bed to catch my breath and finally tore open the paper to see what I'd "bought" with my dime. What a surprise I had!"

The children waited for a few seconds as Daddy sipped on his coffee, but they knew that they were going to have to ask.

"Well, Gaga, what was in the package?!"

Daddy smiled his biggest, lifted his coffee cup to his mouth to drain the last drop of cold coffee, pushed himself away from the table and, with a Santa Claus twinkle in his eyes replied, "Oh, just a bunch of baloney – like all the rest of these stories."

Epilogue

I hope that this book, has made you more aware of, or cause you to seek out, your own family legends – the stars and the supporting cast. And, whether or not you have a big round table in your home, perhaps some evening or Sunday afternoon, you will be inspired to turn off your "big flat screen TV" in order to talk among yourselves about those legends. Keeping alive the memories of the people and the experiences that help to shape who we are is the closest we'll get to immortality. (And that is no baloney!)

Acknowledgments

In 1985, five years after my father died, the immediate family still talked about his stories. While we suspected they might live on as "oral history," we wanted a written record that would capture his style and ensure the longevity of the stories and his spirit. We also suspected that others might enjoy them as much as we had. I chose to create the written record, but I couldn't have done it alone. As the family reminisced about the stories, forgotten details emerged, and, as those details came together, it was like watching, in my mind's eye, an audio-visual presentation of sitting at the "big round table," and that mental image allowed the words, the stories, to flow easily onto paper.

I printed out copies of the stories in amateurish manuscript form. Over the years the copies have been distributed to family members and old friends and colleagues of Daddy's. But now, in the 21st century, with easy opportunities for wider distribution, my brother, John R. Lutes, II (Johnny, to me), encouraged me to take that step, motivated by the fact that his own son, John R. Lutes, III, never had the opportunity to sit around the big round table in Gaga's presence. Also, in August 2010, Johnny began to experience the joy and privilege of being a grandfather when Jack (the original John R. Lutes's lifelong nickname) was born. Johnny doesn't want Jack's image of his great-grandfather to be only a faded photo. He wants it to be as fun and lively and creative as the man himself.

Having four grandsons of my own, I happily responded to Johnny's encouragement, a gift that allowed me to spend time with memories of my family as, once again, I watched and listened to the audio-visual presentation in my mind.

One of the amazing advantages of working in a university, as I do, is that one is surrounded by experts in diverse fields and several of them came to my aid when I took on the task of preparing Daddy's stories for publication. Though I personally believe the stories can entertain anyone of any age, I thank those in Samford's School of Education (David Little and his colleagues) for using software to determine the reading level of the book.

Nancy Whitt, recently retired Chair of Samford's English department, generously accepted my request to proofread and make comments on the original manuscript (claiming it to be a pleasure to read something that she didn't have to grade). It was her suggestion that I bring as much life and clarity to the setting (the big round table) as my father had brought to his stories. Once again the audio-visual mental presentation came in handy. All I had to do is simply describe the details that I could so clearly see in my mind. With his typical thoroughness and generosity, English professor and author and editor (and good friend), Chris Metress, kindly did the final proofreading.

Finally, when creating the author's picture for the back cover, I was fully aware of the fact that Daddy was the true author, even though I had put the words to paper. I had an idea that would represent our "co-authorship." I described my idea to Joe Zellner, of Samford's Technology Learning Center, and the deed was done before the day was over.

So several levels of family were involved in the publication of this little book of tall tales. The heirs and ancestors of John R. Lutes. His family of friends (fellow salesmen and customers) who enjoyed his story telling talents as much as we did. My Samford "family" who so generously lent their know-how to the effort. And, of

Acknowledgements

course, at the center of it all was Daddy, the story-teller, and Mother, his devoted supporter in all that he did.